Dear Parents,

Welcome to the Scholastic Reader s̶ ̶ ̶ ̶ ̶ ̶ ̶ ̶ ̶ ̶ ̶ ̶ ̶ ̶)
years of experience with teachers, parents, and children and put it
into a program that is designed to match your child's interests
and skills.

Level 1—Short sentences and stories made up of words kids
can sound out using their phonics skills and words that are
important to remember.

Level 2—Longer sentences and stories with words kids need
to know and new "big" words that they will want to know.

Level 3—From sentences to paragraphs to longer stories, these
books have large "chunks" of texts and are made up of a rich
vocabulary.

Level 4—First chapter books with more words and fewer
pictures.

It is important that children learn to read well enough to succeed
in school and beyond. Here are ideas for reading this book with
your child:

• Look at the book together. Encourage your child to read the
  title and make a prediction about the story.
• Read the book together. Encourage your child to sound out
  words when appropriate. When your child struggles, you can
  help by providing the word.
• Encourage your child to retell the story. This is a great way
  to check for comprehension.
• Have your child take the fluency test on the last page to check
  progress.

Scholastic Readers are designed to support your child's efforts
to learn how to read at every age and every stage. Enjoy
helping your child learn to read and love to read.

— **Francie Alexander**
    Chief Education Officer
    Scholastic Education

Library of Congress Cataloging-in-Publication Data

Hernandez-Rosenblatt, Jason.
Batman : the purr-fect crime / by Jason Hernandez-Rosenblatt; illustrated
by Rick Burchett.
p. cm. -- (Scholastic reader. Level 3)
"Batman created by Bob Kane."
Summary: When Catwoman tries to outwit Batman and steal two priceless
statues, the Dark Knight has to guess what she might try next.
ISBN 0-439-47100-1 (pbk.)
[1. Heroes--Fiction. 2. Robbers and outlaws--Fiction.] I. Burchett, Rick, ill.
II. Title. III. Series.
PZ7.H432134Bat 2004
[E]--dc22   2003025866

10 9 8 7 6 5 4 3 2   04 05 06 07 08
Printed in the U.S.A. 23 • First printing, June 2004

BATMAN™
THE
PURR-FECT CRIME

Written by **Jason Hernandez-Rosenblatt**

Illustrated by **Rick Burchett**

Batman created by Bob Kane

Scholastic Reader — Level 3

Cartwheel BOOKS®

SCHOLASTIC INC.

New York Toronto London Auckland Sydney
Mexico City New Delhi Hong Kong Buenos Aires

CHAPTER ONE

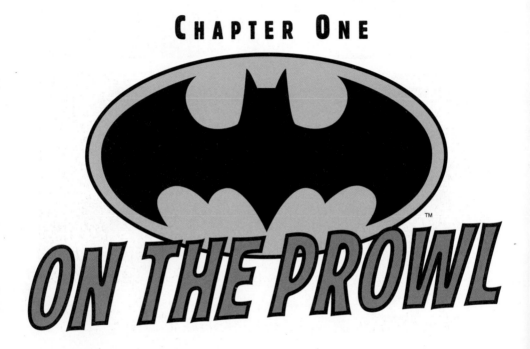

ON THE PROWL

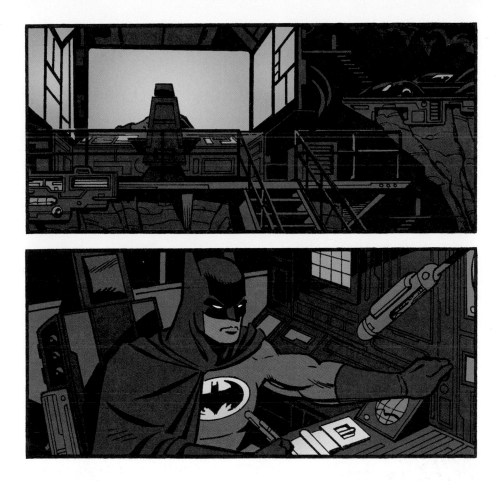

Bruce Wayne was one of the richest men in Gotham City. He lived in Wayne Manor, above a secret cave — the Batcave!

That's because Bruce was also Batman!

Every evening, Batman carefully checked his crime-fighting tools and equipment. Then he would go out on patrol.

On the roof of the Gotham Museum, Catwoman was so happy she could purr.

But she was as quiet as she could be. It was the middle of the night. Any noise could set off the alarms outside. And that would bring Batman!

IT WAS MIDNIGHT AT THE GOTHAM CITY MUSEUM...

Catwoman carefully cut a hole into the glass skylight with her glass cutter. The hole was just big enough for her to wiggle through.

She smiled as she dropped a rope through the hole. Quiet as a cat, she went down the rope into the dark museum.

The week before, she had stolen the plans for the museum's alarm system from the security company. So she knew just what she would find.

Four feet below her was a maze of hidden laser beams. If anything passed through any one of the beams, it would trigger the alarm.

So Catwoman pulled a small spray can from a bag on her belt. She sprayed the floor.

A cloud of smoke spread through the darkness. The beams of light shone bright red!

Catwoman dropped safely to the floor between the beams, like a cat who always lands on her feet.

Step one was done. It was time for step two.

Inside the glass display case in front of her were the very things she had come to the museum to steal—the Golden Cats of Bast!

CHAPTER TWO

A TAIL OF THREE CATS

Catwoman could not resist a valuable cat. And the twin statues of Bast, an ancient Egyptian goddess in the shape of a cat, were worth a lot of money. The statues, on loan from the Egyptian government, were solid gold, with glowing rubies for eyes and collars with big diamonds.

THE GOLDEN CATS OF BAST!

THE DISPLAY CASE AND THE ALARM WERE FROZEN SOLID!

But Catwoman knew there was an alarm on the display case. And the slightest touch to the case would set it off.

So she pulled out a second spray can. She sprayed the thick glass with a special freezing gas. A mist settled on the case.

Within seconds, the case and the alarm were frozen solid!

Catwoman tapped the glass. The case broke into pieces! With a happy purr, Catwoman picked up the first statue.

Once, Catwoman had been a lonely little girl named Selina Kyle. And cats were her only friends.

Then she decided to become a super-villain. She chose the name Catwoman and dressed as a cat for her secret identity. Catwoman trusted cats, not people.

"Purr-fect!" said Catwoman as she put the first statue into her pouch. But as she reached for the second one, she heard a familiar voice.

"Sorry to spoil your night, Catwoman." And then the lights came on!

SUDDENLY, SHE HEARD A FAMILIAR VOICE!

CHAPTER THREE

NINE LIVES

"Batman!" she hissed. She whirled around.

"How did you know? I was so careful!"

The Caped Crusader stepped from the shadows into the light.

"I only had to wait for you," he said. "As soon as I heard about the Bast exhibit, I knew Catwoman wouldn't be able to resist trying to steal the statues."

"Try?" said Catwoman. "I've got one! And you can't catch me!"

Then Catwoman leaped for the rope that

BATMAN FOLLOWED AS SHE CLAWED HER WAY UP THE ROPE!

still hung from the skylight. Agile as a cat, she began to climb. But the Dark Knight was right behind her.

As Catwoman pulled herself through the hole in the skylight, she could see him climbing after her.

But he would never make it in time to stop her. As soon as she was on the roof, Catwoman untied the rope.

She watched with a smile as the rope fell down the hole. Batman landed with a *THUD!*

"We'll meet again soon, Catwoman!" shouted Batman.

CATWOMAN LET GO OF THE ROPE.

Catwoman didn't want to leave behind the second statue. But she had no choice.

"Batman is always one step ahead of me," she thought as she leaped across the rooftops. "How does he always know where I am?"

Then she remembered something. Batman expected *Catwoman* to steal the statues.

"What if I were *not* Catwoman?" she thought as she escaped into the night.

CHAPTER FOUR

CAT GOT YOUR TONGUE?

Batman sat at the master control center in the Batcave. He looked at the giant computer monitor.

Alfred, his butler and lifelong friend, stepped out of the elevator carrying a tray.

"Here you are, sir," Alfred said. He put the tray down next to Batman. "I trust the night went well?"

"Not at all," Batman said. "Catwoman escaped with one of the statues."

"She is rather a sneaky one," Alfred said.

"Yes, she is," said Batman. "But I can usually guess where she'll strike next."

"She'll try to steal the second statue, of course," said Alfred.

"She'll try," said Batman. "She'll certainly try!"

CHAPTER FIVE

HERE, KITTY, KITTY!

Two days later, Batman was at the Egyptian Embassy in Gotham City where the second Bast statue was being returned for safekeeping. In a little while, an armored car would pull up in front of the building. Police officers would carry a safe with the statue inside it into the embassy.

Batman knew Catwoman would try to steal the statue. But he was ready for her.

He made sure this event was on the news. And he hid inside the guardhouse on a busy street.

Exactly on time, the armored car drove up to the embassy surrounded by four police cars.

Through a crack in the guardhouse door, Batman saw the cars stop in front of the embassy.

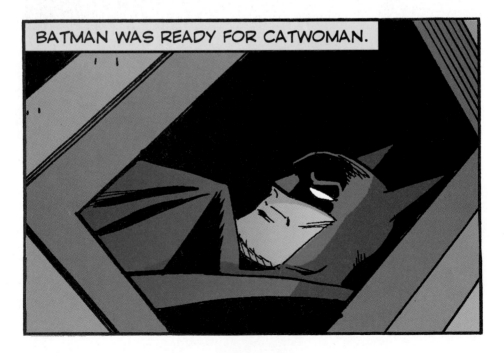

BATMAN WAS READY FOR CATWOMAN.

BATMAN WATCHED FROM HIS HIDING PLACE.

He watched as the Egyptian Ambassador came out of the embassy to meet the armored car.

A policeman and a policewoman pulled the special safe out of the car.

CATWOMAN COULD NEVER RESIST A GOOD CAT CRIME!

Then, following the ambassador, the police officers hurried inside the embassy, carrying the safe.

There was no sign of Catwoman anywhere!

"Where could she be?" Batman thought. "She could never resist a good cat crime!"

Batman was trying to understand his mistake when the armored car drove away, followed by three police cars.

He was about to leave the guardhouse when he saw the policewoman run out of the embassy alone. She hopped into the fourth police car and sped away.

"Didn't the policewoman go into the

embassy with her partner and the ambassador?" Batman wondered. "Where are they?"

He rushed into the embassy and found both men on the floor. The open safe lay between them. It was empty!

Then Batman smelled knockout gas. "Catwoman!" he said.

BATMAN SMELLED KNOCKOUT GAS!

CHAPTER SIX

CAT'S OUT OF THE BAG

CATWOMAN HAD OUTSMARTED BATMAN!

Catwoman purred as she drove away from the embassy. The second gold statue sat on the seat next to her.

She couldn't remember the last time she had been this happy. She had outsmarted Batman! And now both statues were hers!

But how had she done it?

Catwoman had realized she had to steal the statue not as Catwoman but as plain old Selina Kyle.

That morning, she had put on a policewoman's uniform over her costume.

She had taken the place of the policewoman who was supposed to help carry the statue. Then she had walked right past Batman.

Catwoman knew Batman must have been near the embassy, watching. But she also knew he had been looking for Catwoman, not Selina Kyle.

A POLICE CAR HAS BEEN STOLEN!

Catwoman purred again as she drove through Gotham's streets. Suddenly, the car radio crackled on.

"This is Batman! A police car has been stolen. It was last seen headed east on Sprang Avenue!"

But Catwoman wasn't worried. She knew Batman would figure out what had happened. She had planned for that.

She made several turns through the busy city streets. She made sure no one was following her.

Then she drove into a deserted alley.

SHE HAD A PLAN!

There, the feline felon threw away the stolen policewoman's uniform. She was Catwoman once again.

Then, clutching the statue, she climbed a fire escape and ran across the rooftops toward home.

CATWOMAN...

...LEAPED ACROSS ROOFTOPS TOWARD HOME.

CHAPTER SEVEN

CAT-NAB!

Suddenly, the Dark Knight stepped from behind a chimney into Catwoman's path!

"Batman!" she screeched like a cat whose tail had been stepped on.

"Nice try, Catwoman," Batman said. "Maybe you can run from the police, but you can't escape my Bat-tracer. It led me right to you!"

"Bat-tracer?" Catwoman said, confused.

Batman pointed to the gold statue. Catwoman turned it over. There she saw a small blinking object.

"An electronic tracking device!" Batman said.

"No!" howled Catwoman.

She hissed and threw the statue at Batman. Then she started running the other way.

Batman caught the priceless statue with

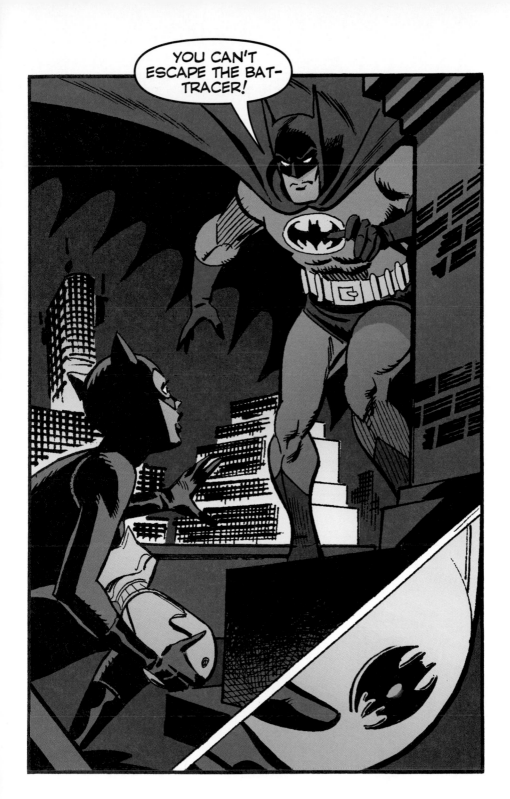

NO MATTER WHAT, CATWOMAN COULD NOT GET AWAY!

one hand. With his other hand, he threw a
Batarang that wrapped a rope around
Catwoman's feet. She fell down hard onto
the rooftop.

A moment later, the dark shape of
Batman stood over her, snapping the
Batcuffs on her wrists.

"I thought I had finally outsmarted you,

Batman," said Catwoman.

"You almost did," said Batman. "But you should know better than anyone that a leopard can't change her spots!"

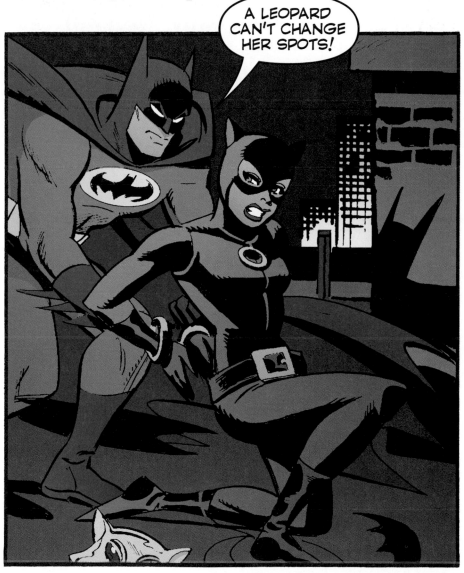

Fluency Fun

The words in each list below end in the same sounds.
Read the words in a list.
Read them again.
Read them faster.
Try to read all 15 words in one minute.

night	**carefully**	**foil**
right	**lonely**	**soil**
bright	**safely**	**broil**
skylight	**suddenly**	**spoil**
tonight	**usually**	**turmoil**

Look for these words in the story.

museum	**statue**	**ancient**
building	**special**	

Note to Parents:

According to *A Dictionary of Reading and Related Terms*, fluency is "the ability to read smoothly, easily, and readily with freedom from word-recognition problems." Fluency is necessary for good comprehension and enjoyable reading. The activities on this page include a speed drill and a sight-recognition drill. Speed drills build fluency because they help students rapidly recognize common syllables and spelling patterns in words, and they're fun! Sight-recognition drills help students smoothly and accurately recognize words. Practice these activities with your child to help him or her become a fluent reader.

—**Wiley Blevins,**
Reading Specialist